WILD MIDNIGHT

AN EMILY STORY

Book design by Jake Nordby
Illustrations by Jomike Tejido

Published in the United States by Jolly Fish Press, an imprint of North Star Editions, Inc.

First Edition
First Printing, 2018

This is a work of fiction. Names, characters, places, and incidents are either the product of the author's imagination or are used fictitiously, and any resemblance to actual persons living or dead, business establishments, events, or locales is entirely coincidental.

Library of Congress Cataloging-in-Publication Data (pending)
978-1-63163-157-3 (paperback)
978-1-63163-156-6 (hardcover)

Jolly Fish Press
North Star Editions, Inc.
2297 Waters Drive
Mendota Heights, MN 55120
www.jollyfishpress.com

Printed in the United States of America

SECOND CHANCE
RANCH

WILD
MIDNIGHT

AN EMILY STORY

KELSEY ABRAMS

ILLUSTRATED BY JOMIKE TEJIDO

TEXT BY LAURIE J. EDWARDS

JOLLY
FiSH
PRESS

Mendota Heights, Minnesota

Chapter One

Emily sniffled and put a bookmark in the book she was reading. *That poor little horse. All it wanted was to live in the wild, but they captured it and took it away from its mother.*

Her twin sister, Grace, burst into the room, fanning herself with one hand. "Whew, it's hot out there." She took a sip from her purple water bottle and crossed the room. As she neared Emily's bed, she slid to a halt. "Are you crying?"

"Noo . . ." *Not really.* Sniffling didn't count as crying, did it?

Grace swiped a finger under Emily's eye and waved it in front of her sister's face. "Then why is my finger wet?" Grace asked in a triumphant voice.

"Well, maybe I was a little," Emily admitted. Her sister would keep pestering until she had an explanation for the tears so, heaving a sigh, Emily said, "I'm reading a story about mustangs that run wild and how they're rounded up and sold off. I just read the part about a helicopter swooping in to scare them, so men on horseback could capture them. One was a baby, and they took him away from his mom."

"That sounds sad." Grace jumped on the bed and picked up the book. She never just sat on a bed, she bounced up and down. It made Emily seasick—if it was possible to be seasick on land. "Why read it if it makes you cry?"

"I hope it has a happy ending," Emily said. "The other books in this series do."

Flipping the book over, Grace read the back cover. "It doesn't say what happens at the end. But the author owns mustangs she rescued, so I guess she knows what she's talking about."

"She does? I didn't read that part. Let me see." Emily took the book from her sister and read the back cover. "Look at this—she has a website for herself, but there's also one for the mustangs. I'm going to go check it out." She headed for the family room to use the computer, and Grace trailed after her.

Grace's cat, Chances, followed them down the hall, meowing, until Grace picked up the fluffy white Persian and scratched her behind the ears. "I wanted you to come outside and play soccer with me," Grace said to Emily.

"Thought you said it was hot," Emily said.

"Not too hot to play soccer. Besides, you don't have to do anything," Grace said. "Just jump around in front of the goal while I shoot."

Sighing heavily, Emily sat in the desk chair and turned on the computer. "No, thanks." The last time she'd played goalie, Grace had drilled a ball right into Emily's stomach. Not on purpose, but still . . .

"Aww, Em, you know that was an accident," Grace defended herself. "I wasn't trying to hit you. My foot slipped."

Pictures of the wild mustangs popped up on the Bureau of Land Management's website, and Emily clicked on the gallery to see all the mustangs. "Here they are. These are all the ones they've rounded up for adoption."

"Why do they round them up?" Grace asked. "How come they don't just let them stay wild?"

Emily clicked on the online gallery of the city closest to them before answering. "In the book, the rescuers said there's not enough grass to feed all of them. If they don't find homes, the horses won't have enough food."

Grace leaned in for a closer look. "Ooo . . . I like that one. And that one. And look at this one with the white on its face. And the black one."

Emily tilted her head to the side to see where Grace was pointing, but her sister's head blocked her view. Grace usually got overly enthusiastic about things. "Um, Grace," Emily said, "you're in my way. I can't see anything."

Grace backed up a little. "Sorry, but they're just so cute. Which one are you going to adopt?"

Emily studied them one by one, and her sister was right. They were all so beautiful. It would be hard to pick only one. "I guess I should check out what I

have to do." She clicked on the requirements, and her heart sank. "You have to be eighteen or older. Do you think Mom and Dad would do it for me?"

"Sure, why not? They let the rest of us adopt animals in need. Why wouldn't they let you help one of the mustangs?" Grace offered.

Grace's breezy answer calmed Emily. "Okay, so let me read the rest of the information," Emily said. They had a lot of rules about corrals, shelters, and transportation. She took a notepad from the desk and jotted down the important points. Near the bottom of the page, she stopped. "What's this about payment?" She checked around on the site. "Oh, you have to bid on them, and the auction is closing soon."

That night at dinner, Emily's anxiety about her parents' response prevented her from asking about the mustang auction. Grace kept elbowing Emily, but every time she got up her courage to speak, someone else started talking.

"When are you going to ask?" Grace's whisper was loud enough for everyone to hear.

Mrs. Ramirez raised an eyebrow. "Did you have something you wanted to ask, Emily?"

Emily nodded and launched into an explanation. Once she got started, she became so enthusiastic her nervousness went away. She described several of the horses, and Grace chimed in about her favorites.

Their twelve-year-old sister, Natalie, leaned in and listened intently. Natalie was crazy about horses. "That would be awesome to rescue a wild mustang," she said.

Emily smiled at her. One of Natalie's jobs was overseeing everyone's chores in the stables. If Natalie got excited about the idea, she might help to convince Mom and Dad to bid on one.

"Well," Mr. Ramirez said when she'd finished, "I guess we'll have to look at the site after dinner to see what we need to do."

"I have the information right here." Emily waved the notepad with her notes on it.

Mrs. Ramirez smiled. "Seems like you're really prepared, but let's finish dinner first."

Emily set her notes down with a sigh. All she wanted to do was talk about the mustangs. The last thing she wanted to do was eat dinner.

Natalie was a good cook, but she liked to make spicy dishes when she helped out in the kitchen. Tonight it was chiles rellenos. Grace insisted the poblano peppers inside the outer crust tasted mild, but even with the cheese filing, they stung Emily's tongue and made her eyes water. Although they were twins, she and Grace often had the exact opposite reactions to things. Reluctantly, Emily cut a small bite and put it in her mouth, then picked up her water glass to wash it down.

She was a macaroni-and-cheese kind of eater. The blander the better. She even preferred plain macaroni with butter on it to spaghetti with sauce, and so did her ten-year-old sister, Abby, although for different reasons. Abby was on the autism spectrum, so she liked her foods mild and in separate places on her plate, with nothing touching anything else. She also disliked loud noises and bright lights, but her responses to these things improved when she got her service dog, Amigo.

Maybe if Emily got her mustang, she could have a close animal friend like Amigo or Grace's cat, Chances. Emily loved their emu, Chandler, and could pet him and talk to him. But emus weren't cuddly like cats and dogs. And they didn't have soft coats she could lean against, and couldn't talk to them the way she could horses. Although she'd probably not get to do that with a wild mustang. At least not at first.

Emily was so engrossed in her daydreams about mustangs that she was startled when she noticed everyone in her family was staring at her. "What?" she said.

"We're waiting for you to finish, Em," Grace said, pointing at Emily's almost-full plate.

No one left the table at the Ramirez house until everyone was done eating. The rest of the family

had cleaned their plates already, and they were all waiting for her.

"Oh, sorry." Emily shoveled a big bite into her mouth, and tears sprang to her eyes. She wished it were a night Mom had cooked instead of Natalie.

Mom had explained that Abby's senses were more easily overwhelmed than other people's, so new experiences or strong sounds, tastes, and lights bothered her. Mom had also found some articles on supertasters and suggested Emily might be one. Supertasters had extra taste buds. They could taste bitterness or spiciness even in foods that others thought were mild. When Mom cooked, she often made the bland things Emily and Abby preferred. Grace and Natalie doused Mom's meals with hot sauce or fiery salsas. But there wasn't a way to make hot things less spicy.

With everyone staring at her, Emily managed to choke down the rest of her meal with many gulps of water. She reminded herself that the faster she finished, the faster they could talk about the mustangs.

When Emily finished her last bite, Mr. Ramirez said, "Why don't we skip dessert for now so we can look at the information Emily found?" He set his napkin on the table and stood. "Maybe we could have s'mores later under the stars."

Natalie smiled, and Grace cheered. Abby bent to pet Amigo until Grace quieted.

S'mores sounded great, but all Emily wanted was

to discuss the auction. Then she'd enjoy the dessert, especially if Mom and Dad agreed. She hoped they would, but what if they said *no*?

Chapter Two

After everyone set their dishes on the counter, Emily held up the paper with her notes. "I have the most important information on here, but maybe you should look at the website too."

Abby left the room with Amigo to play with one of her favorite dogs, Cocoa, and her two puppies that hadn't been adopted yet. Grace started to head to the family room, but Mr. Ramirez stopped her. "Isn't it your turn to do the dishes tonight?" he asked.

"I want to see the website too," Grace pouted. She turned around and trudged back into the kitchen.

"You already did," Emily pointed out as she spread the papers on the kitchen table. "By the time you're done with the dishes, Mom and Dad will have looked at everything, and there'll be more room for you at the computer."

"I guess." Grace absentmindedly squirted dish-washing liquid into the sink. "Can't I do the dishes later?" she whined as she turned the hot water on full blast. "I want to see the mustangs too."

Emily gave her a sympathetic glance as her parents glanced over her notes.

"I suppose," Mr. Ramirez said. "As long as you don't forget to come back here afterwards."

"Yay!" Grace jumped up and down. "You should see the mustangs they have on the site." She launched into a long description of her favorite ones.

Mrs. Ramirez looked up from Emily's notes and screeched, "Grace! The sink!"

Suds overflowed the sink and bubbled onto the counter and floor. Grace turned around and snapped off the faucet. "I-I'm sorry."

Natalie raced for the mop and bucket. Mrs. Ramirez and Emily grabbed rags. Mr. Ramirez moved as close to the sink as he could without stepping in the puddle forming below the counter and opened the drain.

"How much soap did you put in?" he asked in a quiet voice.

"I don't know." Grace looked close to tears. "I wasn't paying attention."

Mrs. Ramirez sighed and threw an old towel on the floor near Mr. Ramirez's feet. "Can you lift her onto that so she can dry her feet?" she asked her husband.

After Mr. Ramirez picked up Grace, the other three set to work cleaning up the water and suds.

"I'm sorry." Grace's chin wobbled, and she looked about to cry.

Emily felt sorry for her sister. Grace had a hard time thinking before acting, so she often caused problems or accidents. But not on purpose.

"It's okay, Grace," Emily said. "You didn't mean to do it." She picked up another sopping-wet cloth and wrung it out over the mop bucket.

Grace gave her a grateful look, and Emily pushed aside the thought that this was delaying everyone from seeing her mustang site. Cleaning this mess up was more important.

Once they had the floor cleaned up, Grace put

the dishes in the right amount of soapy water. She stayed behind to finish the washing up while Emily led the way to the family room computer.

On the way, Emily recapped the key points. When they got to the computer, she pulled up the government website and stepped out of the way so her parents could read the information. Natalie peeked over their shoulders.

After they'd looked it over, Emily convinced her parents to sign up so they could bid. They printed out the forms and read through them. Then Mr. Ramirez filled them out and sketched the required map of their ranch on the second page. In the box beside that, he drew pictures of the corral and barn layouts. By that time, Mrs. Ramirez had addressed the envelope, filled out the deposit check, and taken a stamp out of the desk drawer.

"I'll mail this on my way to work tomorrow," she promised after she'd slipped the completed application into the envelope.

Emily could hardly contain her excitement. They still had to wait for the approval of their facility, but they'd already made a start. Once their ranch had been okayed, she could start bidding.

By the time a subdued Grace joined them, they were discussing how much they could afford to pay. Her parents came up with a top bid. Emily agreed to stick to it.

While Mr. Ramirez went out to start a blaze in the fire pit to toast marshmallows, Emily and Grace looked over the horses on the computer. Natalie gave them suggestions. Working together, they selected several favorites.

"I like this one best," Natalie said.

Emily nodded. It wasn't her top pick, but Natalie knew the most about horses, so Emily decided to go with that one. But when they looked at the bids, that horse was already out of their price range, so Emily chose a different horse to bid on. She'd fallen in love with a black mustang, and the bidding was still low.

"I'm keeping my fingers crossed it stays low so I can bid on it once we're approved."

Emily could hardly contain her excitement as she headed out back for s'mores. But it was nothing compared to Grace's jumping around as all four sisters gathered supplies in the kitchen.

"I can't wait to see if we win the bid!" Grace babbled. "A new horse, s'mores, and no school tomorrow." She flung her arms out in the air, almost hitting Natalie, who'd just emerged from the pantry carrying the s'more ingredients.

Natalie took one look at Grace and handed her the bag of marshmallows. They usually avoided giving Grace breakable things when she was as excited as this. The worst that could happen to the marshmallows was that Grace might fall on the bag and squish them. Luckily, she was pretty steady on her feet.

Emily grabbed the chocolate bars, and Abby took the box of graham crackers.

"I'll be right out," Natalie said, "as soon as I get the skewers and some napkins."

They all, except for Abby, pulled their chairs close to the crackling blaze. Abby arranged her chocolate, marshmallows, and graham crackers in neat piles on a napkin spread on the wooden table beside her chair.

Mr. Ramirez calmed Grace down before letting her toast her first marshmallow. Hers caught on fire almost immediately, and she blew on it to put it out. She slid her charred marshmallow between two graham crackers with a square of chocolate inside.

Emily held her own marshmallow above the flames and rotated it slowly until it was light brown on all sides. Then she carefully constructed her chocolate–graham cracker sandwich with the perfectly toasted marshmallow. The hot, gooey marshmallow and melted chocolate filled her mouth as she crunched down on the graham crackers. *Yum!* She closed her eyes and enjoyed every bite. Supertasters had no trouble at all with sweets.

They stayed outside talking until the stars came out. Mom always enjoyed pointing out constellations.

Abby remembered them best. She was a whiz at anything to do with math, patterns, or memorizing.

Emily thought it was a perfect evening—time with her family, a delicious snack, and maybe, just maybe, a wild mustang of her own.

Emily spent a few tense days waiting for their ranch's clearance to come through. The minute it was approved, she double-checked all the horses to be sure the black one was still the right mustang for her. Once she chose a horse, she would not be able to switch and bid on a different one. Emily wanted to be absolutely certain about her choice.

She asked her sisters and parents to look at her favorites and give their opinions. Her black one got the most votes, and the bidding was still low. Emily took a deep breath and, following the rules about bidding, placed her first bid. Her stomach clenched as she pushed the button to okay it.

She turned to Grace. "I did it. I really did it."

Grace smiled. "You spent a lot of time picking that one. I never would have been that patient."

Then Emily turned to Natalie. "Do you think I made the right choice?" She valued her older sister's opinion.

"You made the right choice for you," Natalie

assured her. "That's the best horse for the money. I hope you get him."

Emily did too.

Each day after school, she'd check the bidding and the price rose higher and higher. Emily upped her bid each time until she reached the limit—and was outbid once more.

"Please can I go higher?" she begged.

Mrs. Ramirez shook her head. "I'm afraid not. We have to feed the animals we have and pay bills." She slipped an arm around Emily's shoulders. "I'm so sorry, sweetie. Maybe we'll have better luck next year."

Mr. Ramirez patted her shoulder. "I'm sure we will."

But that didn't stop the pain of losing her dream. "I-I'm going upstairs," Emily said, fighting back tears. Sometimes losing herself in a book helped.

Grace stopped Emily from climbing the stairs. "Don't worry," Grace said. "We'll find a way to get you a horse."

"Thanks, Grace, but I'll figure it out." Emily didn't say it aloud, but her sister's hare-brained schemes often got them into trouble. Grace meant well but didn't always think before rushing into action. Besides, not just any horse would do. She had to find a way to get a wild mustang.

Chapter Three

Emily struggled to keep her mind on her chores the next afternoon. Even feeding and caring for her emu didn't perk her up.

"I didn't get the mustang I bid on," she whispered to Chandler.

He seemed to understand and sympathize. Although Chandler let her hug him and lean her head against his soft feathers, it only made her sadder.

After she finished her jobs, she went on the website to look up the horse she'd wanted before she got started on some homework. She wondered if his new owner would love him as much as she would have.

Natalie came into the family room to watch one of her favorite DVDs and passed Emily at the computer. "So sorry about the mustang, Em. I know it hurts."

Emily managed a wan smile. "Thanks." Not long ago, Natalie had to give up Tango, a horse she'd fallen in love with, so she knew her older sister really did understand.

A few days later, Mrs. Ramirez came home after working at Sugarberry Animal Hospital and knocked on Emily and Grace's bedroom door. Emily sat at her desk painting a picture of Chandler. She'd pinned a photo on her bulletin board of Chandler in a funny pose, and she was trying to capture the spirit of it in her painting. Painting helped her keep her mind off her disappointment.

When Emily said, *come in*, Mrs. Ramirez stuck her head around the door.

"I don't want to disturb you if you're busy painting," Mrs. Ramirez said, "but I have some news I thought you might find interesting."

Emily dipped her paintbrush into her water dish to rinse it out and set it on a paper towel. "It's okay. My painting isn't going well. I can't get Chandler's expression right."

Mrs. Ramirez came over and studied the photo. "That's hilarious." Then she looked down at the papers spread across the desk. She tapped a finger on one of the sketches. "Looks like you have the expression here."

"Yeah, but when I try to paint it, Chandler's face looks stiff and frozen," Emily explained.

"Keep trying. You'll get it." Mrs. Ramirez patted her shoulder.

Emily had been trying since she got home from school but hadn't gotten it right yet. It was hard to get a comical pose down on paper when she was feeling glum.

Mrs. Ramirez went over and sat on Emily's bed. She kicked off her shoes and curled her legs under her. "I had some patients today I thought you might be interested in hearing about."

Hiding her sigh, Emily turned her desk chair to face Mrs. Ramirez, but she couldn't muster up her usual enthusiasm for her mother's animal stories. On the nightstand beside Emily's bed, a partially read book was turned over to mark her place. Emily hadn't touched that book since she'd lost the mustang bid. She couldn't bear to read about mustangs. Not yet.

"So today," Mrs. Ramirez said, "I had an appointment at a ranch not far from here. They'd asked me to come out to check out four horses they'd bought."

Not a horse story. Not today. Please, Mom.

"Anyway," Mrs. Ramirez continued, "when I got there, the horses turned out to be mustangs. Wild mustangs."

Emily sucked in a breath. Just hearing the word *mustang* made her whole body ache. Why was her mom doing this when she knew how much losing that mustang hurt?

"They got their mustangs from the auction you bid in. One of them is pure black like the one you wanted. I don't think it's the same one, but it looks similar." Mrs. Ramirez gave Emily a sympathetic smile.

Blinking back tears, Emily fixed her gaze on her

bare toes as they traced the diamond shapes on the Navajo rug covering the wide-plank floors.

"Here's the best part," Mrs. Ramirez said. "I told them about you and how much you'd wanted a wild mustang, and they said you could come over anytime to watch them work with the horses." She reached into her pocket and pulled out a card. "Here's their number if you want to give them a call."

Emily took the card Mrs. Ramirez held out. "Thanks." She wasn't sure whether she could handle watching other people working with mustangs, but her mom had been kind to think of it and to get their contact information.

Mrs. Ramirez stood and walked over to Emily. She gave her shoulders a quick squeeze. "I know it's not the same as having a mustang of your own, sweetie, but maybe you can pick up some tips on training them for when you do get one."

Emily's tears threatened to overflow as she hugged her mom back. She already had a pony of her own and the other horses they'd adopted. Plus she had a family who loved her. She tried to concentrate on that instead of her sadness, but it wasn't easy.

"You know . . ." Mrs. Ramirez stopped on her way out the door. "I've been thinking. Natalie started cooking when she was nine. Maybe it's time you and Grace started taking turns."

Emily suspected Mom had said that to get her

mind off the mustangs, but it worked. She tried to picture her and Grace making meals. "Do you think that's safe? I mean, Grace does get a bit, um, distracted sometimes."

Mrs. Ramirez smiled. "That's why I thought you could work with her."

As much as Emily loved her sister, she couldn't see the two of them fixing meals together. A picture of the kitchen going up in flames flashed in front of Emily's eyes. "I don't know," Emily said. "Besides, nobody would want to eat what I like."

"Abby will like it, and it wouldn't hurt everyone else in the family to experiment." Mrs. Ramirez's lips quirked. "It might also help you to become a little more adventurous in your meal choices."

"I'll think about it," Emily said.

"Good," Mrs. Ramirez said as she stepped into the hallway. "I've put the two of you on the kitchen rotation schedule for next Tuesday. Get together with Grace to plan the menu and be sure to put all the ingredients you'll need on the grocery list before we go shopping on Saturday."

Emily had meant she'd think about doing it someday. Not next week. How could she and Grace possibly plan and prepare a meal so soon? "Umm . . . Mom?" Emily asked.

It was too late. Mrs. Ramirez had already closed the door.

Oh, great. Emily tossed the card her mom had given her onto her nightstand beside her unread book, but the card drifted to the floor. Usually she picked things up and kept her half of the room neat, unlike Grace's side, where clothes and sports equipment were scattered everywhere. Today, though, she didn't bother. She'd get it later.

Emily was flicking her paintbrush in short, rapid strokes to form the spiky fur around the emu's head when the bedroom door opened again—this time with a bang. She jumped and paint splattered over the picture. She sighed. At least it was one where she hadn't quite captured Chandler's expression.

"What's the matter, Em?" Grace hurried over to the desk and peered over Emily's shoulder. "Aww . . . was that my fault?"

"The door startled me," Emily said.

"I'm sorry. I was so excited because I drilled ten shots in a row into the upper left corner of the net." Grace mimed a kicking motion with her foot.

Pushing aside her own disappointment, Emily used her most enthusiastic tone. "Wow! That's great!" Grace had been working hard for weeks to master that shot.

"Yeah, I know. I was coming to see if you wanted to watch me." Grace's shoulders slumped a bit, and she gestured toward the painting. "I guess not."

Emily rinsed out her brush again. "Watch you, yes. Play goalie, no."

Grace's cheeks reddened. "I'm sorry about kicking that ball into your stomach and about this." Grace pointed to the paint spatters.

"I know you are." Emily set down her brush and slid back her chair. "Okay, let's go see this killer soccer shot."

"You're done painting?" Grace asked, hopefully.

"It wasn't going well even before the splash marks, so taking a break might be good," Emily said.

"Yay!" Grace headed for the door but stopped as she passed Emily's nightstand. "What's that on the floor?" She pounced on the business card.

Emily shook her head. Leave it to Grace to spot one small thing on Emily's side of the room when her own side was filled with junk.

Grace read the card. "Are we getting another horse?"

"I wish." Emily took the card from her sister. "Mom gave it to me because that ranch bought some wild mustangs to train."

"They did? Can you go over to see them?" Grace asked. "That would be so cool."

Chances stalked into the room, rubbed against Emily's leg, and then curled up on one of the platforms on the scratching-post tree in the corner of the room. Grace went over and squatted down to pet her cat.

Meanwhile, Emily ran her finger over the raised letters on the card. *Rancho del Sol.* Under it, in small print, it said, *Mustangs bought, sold, and trained.* They'd passed Rancho del Sol on their trail rides, so it wasn't too far to ride there. Maybe she should at least take a look. It might be painful to see someone else with a black mustang, but perhaps she could learn about training wild horses.

Chapter Four

After Emily watched Grace shoot a bunch of goals, she wandered into the kitchen where her older sister was making dinner. "Natalie?"

"Hmm?" Natalie was paging through a cookbook. "This looks delicious, doesn't it?"

Emily gulped. Anything that had jalapeños in it would be hot. She didn't want to hurt her sister's feelings, but it didn't sound good to her.

When she didn't answer, Natalie looked up and smiled. "I guess you weren't the best person to ask about this one."

"Probably not," Emily agreed. "But I have a question for you."

Natalie smoothed out the cookbook pages and then flipped the cookbook over. "What's up?"

"You know Rancho del Sol that we pass on our trail rides? Mom said the owner bought four mustangs." Emily's voice wavered on the last word, and Natalie gave her a sympathetic look. "They said I could come and watch them train them. But we're not allowed to ride alone, so I wondered if you'd come with me on Saturday."

Natalie was quick to agree. "Sure. What time? I planned to practice my barrel racing."

If Emily was going to do it, she'd like to start as early as possible. "Maybe right after chores?" she said.

"Okay. I'd be interested in watching what they do, anyway." Natalie slid on the latex gloves she wore to chop jalapeños. Then she flipped over the cookbook, but she glanced over at Emily. "I'm really sorry about the mustang. I know it has to be hard."

Emily ducked her head and nodded. "Thanks." Emily's eyes watered just thinking about those jalapeños. Maybe her mom's idea about taking a turn at cooking might not be as bad as Emily thought. At least she'd have a non-spicy dish the nights she cooked.

She headed off to feed the emu and the horses. "Hey, Chandler," she said as she brought him fresh water. "Natalie agreed to go with me to the mustang ranch, but I forgot Mom said I should call them first."

The thought of calling a stranger made her stomach hurt. "You know how I feel about calling people, even if I know them," Emily continued. If their ranch phone rang, she didn't answer because she froze up whenever she got on the phone and could never remember what she planned to say. She couldn't imagine trying to talk to someone she didn't know about their mustangs. How would she ever make this phone call?

She moved closer to Chandler and then stood still and quiet to sense the emu's mood. The emu took a few steps in her direction, his signal that he'd accept a hug. Emily put her arms around Chandler's neck and leaned into his soft, feathered body for comfort.

Chandler didn't like human contact for long, so he shook himself, meaning it was time to let go. Emily untangled her arms from around him, freeing him. Then she opened the back gate to allow him to enter into the larger enclosure. She'd read that emus needed to exercise, so she made sure Chandler had at least one chance to stretch and run every day. Then she climbed onto the split-rail fence to watch him enjoy his freedom for a few minutes before she fed the horses.

But the thought of the phone call bothered her so much that she could barely enjoy Chandler's happiness. Why was it she could communicate well with animals but not people? When she was with a person, she could sense that person's needs and feelings, but she couldn't do that on the phone. Maybe that was why talking on the phone was so hard.

As she fed the horses, she thought about asking Grace to make the call for her. Grace loved talking to people, and she had no fears of making a phone call. Before she got too carried away, Emily shook her head. Mrs. Ramirez always insisted the girls take responsibility for themselves. This was something she'd have to do herself.

That night at dinner, Natalie carried in a

steaming casserole dish. The sharp tang from the jalapeño peppers stung Emily's eyes. Why would anyone add peppers to macaroni and cheese? Her stomach was already in knots about the phone call. Adding a mouth-burning meal would be even harder on her stomach.

Beside her, Abby tensed. Emily wanted to comfort her, but they'd both need to eat the meal. Abby bent to pet Amigo, a sign she was distressed.

"I made macaroni and cheese tonight," Natalie announced as she set the dish in the center of the table. "See this toothpick? This part of the casserole has no spices."

"Really?" Emily leaned forward. "It's just plain mac and cheese?"

"Yep." Natalie smiled at her. "I figured you and Abby would prefer it plain."

"We would. Thank you, Natalie." Emily was so relieved about dinner, she took two helpings. But she still had anxiety about the phone call. Today was Wednesday. If she didn't call tonight, she only had a few more days to reach them.

When they went around the table that night sharing things about their day, Abby was super excited about a new dog breed she was researching. "It's called a Bergamasco sheepdog." She held up a picture. "It has three kinds of hair that each look different. Some is like regular dog hair, but the other kinds look like goat hair or matted wool. Their hair can touch the ground by age six."

"It looks like a dust mop or like it has tangled dreadlocks," Grace said. "And where are its eyes?"

"Under this hair." Abby pointed to the picture.

Then she launched into a list of facts about the dog that fascinated Emily. Abby was amazing. She was like a walking encyclopedia on dogs. She could memorize facts and details, and she never forgot them.

When it was Grace's turn, she told about her ten goals in a row that afternoon. After Emily had come out to watch her, Grace had managed another ten in a row. "That top left corner is a great place to shoot if the goalie's right-handed," Grace said, "because most goalies' left sides aren't usually as strong."

Emily almost always waited until last to share her news because it was easier for her to be patient. She told everyone about the ranch Mrs. Ramirez said had wild mustangs. "Natalie and I will be riding out there on Saturday morning," she told her family.

"Wonderful," Mrs. Ramirez said. "I'm sure it wasn't easy for you to call and set that up. We're very proud of you for doing that."

Emily hung her head and mumbled, "I didn't actually call yet."

"But I thought . . ." Mrs. Ramirez looked confused for a minute. "I did tell you they'd like you to call first, didn't I?"

Emily dragged a piece of macaroni around on her plate. Suddenly she didn't want to eat another bite of the meal that had tasted delicious minutes before. She could barely get out the word *yes*.

"Oh, good." Mrs. Ramirez relaxed back in her chair. "They have a huge operation out there, so I didn't want you getting underfoot. I'd suggest calling as soon as possible to be sure Saturday works for them."

The lump of fear in Emily's stomach grew larger. Now her mom would ask her every day until she set up the visit. She barely listened to her mom's descriptions of checking the wild mustangs. And she totally missed Natalie's and Dad's sharing while she tried to picture the phone call.

Dialing the number would be hard enough. But what if when someone answered, she couldn't say anything? That would be so embarrassing.

"Em?" Natalie interrupted her thoughts. "I thought you didn't eat the meals I made because they were too spicy." She stared at Emily's plate with sad eyes. "Don't you like my cooking?"

"Huh?" Emily had a hard time coming back from the imaginary phone call. She looked down at her plate, where she'd chopped the macaroni into tiny pieces. She hadn't meant to hurt Natalie's feelings, especially not when her sister had cooked such a special meal. "I loved it. I really did. It's just that—." She swallowed down the lump blocking her throat. "I, well, I'm scared about making that phone call." She couldn't believe she'd admitted that aloud in front of her whole family.

"I know how hard it is for you, sweetie, but it'll be a good learning experience," Mrs. Ramirez said.

Mr. Ramirez nodded. "You can do it."

"Sure you can, Em," Grace chimed in. "All you

have to do is pick up the phone, dial the number, and say, 'Can we come to visit your horses on Saturday?'"

Easy enough for Grace to do. She wasn't scared to talk to people. Emily's mind went blank when she had to talk to people. Her hands shook, and she couldn't remember what she wanted to say. What if they asked her questions and she couldn't think of an answer?

Emily murmured a *thank you*, but her sister would never understand how difficult it was. She tried to push aside her worries so she could finish her dinner. She wanted to encourage Natalie to make more bland meals, so she cleaned her plate.

Later when Emily and Mr. Ramirez were doing dishes, he scrubbed and rinsed a plate. As he handed it to her to dry, he said, "When you dread something, it's best to get it over with quickly. Then it's not hanging over your head for days."

"Mmm-hmm." Emily rubbed the towel over the plate. That was good advice, but as long as she didn't have to call, she didn't have to face it.

Mr. Ramirez tried to make her feel better by telling her stories of times that he was afraid to do things, but that turned out all right in the end. She appreciated his trying to make her feel better. What she really wanted to know was if he'd ever been afraid and what he'd worried about had actually happened.

After they'd cleared the kitchen, Emily headed

upstairs. The minute she walked through the bedroom door, Grace held out her cell phone.

In her other hand she held the business card. "I've already put in the number, so all we have to do is hit the 'send' button."

Emily backed up a few steps and held up a hand. She wasn't ready for that right now. "Let's wait a while."

"Too late," Grace said, "It's ringing." She shoved the phone at Emily.

"Noo . . ." Emily was still moaning when someone picked up on the other end. With trembling hands, she took the phone from her sister. "H-hello," she managed in a voice barely above a whisper.

Evidently the man didn't hear her, because he repeated *hello* several times, each time more impatient than the last. Emily's nightmare closed in around her, and her mind went blank.

The man huffed into the phone. "Anyone there?" Someone behind him muttered something, and he said, "Probably a telemarketer."

Emily panicked. He couldn't hang up, not yet. She wouldn't be brave enough to call again. "Wait!" Her voice came out so loudly it sounded like she was yelling. She took a deep breath. Stuttering and stammering, she stumbled through an explanation, not sure if her words were coming out in the right order or even if they made sense.

"Oh, right," the man said. "The vet's daughter. When did you say you wanted to come?"

"Saturday," Emily squeaked out. "Umm, morning." She took a deep breath. "If that's okay?"

"That should be fine. We'll see you then." He clicked off the phone, not waiting for her to thank him or say good-bye.

Emily sank onto her bed, the phone beeping in her hand. Grace snatched it and ended the call.

Grace danced around the room. "You did it! See, that wasn't so bad, was it?"

Of course not. If you don't mind having sweaty palms, a pounding heart, and a sick feeling in your stomach. In fact, Emily almost felt as if she might vomit.

"So what did he say?" Grace slid her cell phone back in her pocket. "Can you go?"

Emily could only nod. Now that her nerves were starting to calm, she could breathe more easily. She'd done it. She'd made the call. It was over. And the man had agreed she could come. She had no idea who she'd spoken to or what she'd said, but he'd said *yes* and that was all that mattered.

Relief erased most of the tension, and Emily's mood lifted. "I can go on Saturday."

"Yippee!" Grace bounced around like a cheerleader.

Emily lay back on her bed and closed her eyes for

a minute. Then she sat up. "Did I sound dumb when I talked to him?" She studied her sister's face.

"Maybe a little," Grace admitted. "But who cares? He said you could come, and that's the important thing."

Emily groaned and covered her eyes. "How can I go over there on Saturday and face him? He probably thinks I'm crazy."

"Don't worry about it." Grace waved a hand in the air as if it didn't matter. "He probably won't even remember."

Emily wished she could be as casual as her sister about making mistakes, but she worried about everything, especially other people's reactions and feelings. When she faced that man on Saturday, her shyness would probably tangle up her tongue again. That would only confirm his belief about her.

"Can I go tell Natalie?" Grace asked. "And Mom and Dad? Everyone will be happy you made the call."

"Thanks to you," Emily said. "I never would have done it." Then a thought struck her. "I didn't ask about Natalie coming, did I?"

Grace shook her head and pulled her phone out of her pocket. "Want to call him back?"

"No." Calling a stranger once today was enough to last her for months.

"I bet they wouldn't mind if she comes too."

Emily hoped Grace was right.

Chapter Five

On Saturday morning after their chores, Emily and Natalie saddled up for the ride to Rancho del Sol. Emily still worried about taking an extra person along even though her mom had assured her it would be fine, and she dreaded meeting the man she'd talked to on the phone.

When they arrived, though, everyone was too busy to pay much attention to them. After a curt greeting, a weathered old man waved to a split-rail fence some distance from the ring where a horse was kicking and bucking. "Sit there." He appeared ill at ease around them, and each word seemed to be a struggle.

Emily wondered if he was shy, too, and her heart went out to him. She smiled at him to let him know she understood how hard it was to talk to others. Knowing it was hard for him made it a little easier for her. "Thank you," Emily said.

Natalie stopped him as he headed toward the ring. "Could we take a quick tour of the stables? I'd love to see all the horses."

"I suppose." His clipped answer didn't sound as if they'd welcome two girls poking around the barn.

"We don't have to," Emily said shyly.

"No trouble." He waved toward the barn. "Stay back from the wild ones."

Emily smiled her thanks. She wasn't positive, but she thought his eyes softened a little. Then she followed Natalie into the barn.

"Wow, this place is impressive, isn't it? And so are the horses." Natalie stopped at each stall to examine the horse inside. "I wish we could have a barn like this someday."

Emily was happy with their barn, but she had to agree with her sister about this one being impressive. One horse was bucking and kicking at the extra-thick stable doors. When they reached that stall, Emily stopped and sucked in a breath. What a magnificent mustang!

His deep black coat reminded Emily of the mustang she'd lost. Her throat tightened, first for her loss, but then because she could feel his distress. She closed her eyes and felt his fear. He was uncertain and terrified. Trapped in a tiny space after roaming free. She tried to send him calming messages the way she had with the emu.

"It's all right," Emily whispered as she edged closer to the horse's stall.

"Emily!" Natalie's sharp voice cut through her concentration. "They said not to go near the wild ones. That one seems to be the most dangerous of all. Look how he's kicking and the whites of his eyes are showing."

When the whites of horses' eyes were visible, they were either furious or frightened. Although his battering at the stall door could be anger, Emily didn't get that sense. She had no idea how she knew, but she was positive he wouldn't hurt her. "He's only scared, Nat. I want to try to calm him before he hurts himself."

"Stay back, Emily. You could get hurt."

"Just let me try, please," Emily pleaded. "I think I can help him."

Natalie looked unconvinced.

"Remember Chandler?" Emily asked.

Her sister nodded. Emily was the only one in the family who could get near Chandler for the first few weeks. The emu had let Emily touch him from the start. She'd been able to approach him the very first day and take the leash from around his neck. He even let her pet him.

Natalie frowned. "Okay, but don't get too close."

"I won't get any closer than Midnight wants," Emily said.

"Midnight?" Natalie looked confused. "He doesn't have a nameplate on his door. How do you know that's his name?"

"I don't know his name. That one just came to me, and it seems to fit." Emily turned to her sister.

"Can you please be real quiet and not interrupt me while I try?"

Natalie glanced from Emily to the out-of-control mustang. Natalie's eyes reflected her concern for Emily.

"Please, Nat?" Emily asked again.

"All right. I'll try," Natalie conceded, "but don't get hurt."

Emily closed her eyes again and tried to get back in touch with the horse. The fear, the fighting for freedom overwhelmed her. *Tell me what happened*, she said silently to Midnight. *Is it all right if I call you that?*

The mustang grew even wilder and more agitated. Behind Emily, Natalie gasped. Emily sensed the horse was trying to express his story, all the things that had happened. His squealing tore through Emily. She had to find a way to reach him.

I'm listening, Emily told him silently and tried to absorb his pain. Slowly the high-pitched noises lessened. He seemed to be communicating his sad story with grunts and groans. He stopped smashing his hooves against the stall door.

Emily switched to talking aloud. "You're all right. You're safe here. No one will hurt you," she told the mustang. At least she hoped they wouldn't. She should have asked her mom how they trained their horses at this ranch. Some ranchers did it gently; others forced their will on the horse.

She continued to reassure him until he turned both ears forward. Horses did that if they were focused on observing danger or when they were paying attention. Emily studied Midnight's body. Some of the tension in his body seemed to have dissolved, so he must be checking her out.

She met his eyes and took a step toward him. He snorted and pawed the ground. She inched forward, keeping a close watch on his body language. If he appeared nervous, she stopped and talked to him until she felt his signal to move on. Shuffling one small step at a time, she made it to the stall gate.

"Good boy, Midnight," Emily whispered. "We can be friends." She wished she had a peppermint or an apple. Instead she extended her open hand to the horse. Midnight snorted and peeled back his lips to reveal his teeth.

Behind her, Natalie gasped, but she didn't say a word.

Emily waited a few minutes, talking in a low, soothing voice the whole time. She tried to sense Midnight's mood. He'd moved from fearful to wary. He'd never been around humans before, except for those who had captured him, and he didn't trust them.

Emily tried to send Midnight a message that she

wasn't connected to his captors. "I'm different," she told him. "I won't do anything to hurt you." Gradually he relaxed, and she tried reaching out slowly again. She stood with her arm perfectly still.

He took a tentative step toward her. She remained statue-still while he moved a few more paces forward. He snorted again, and it took all of Emily's willpower not to move or react. She didn't say a word as he sniffed the air around her arm, but she sent kind thoughts. *I promise I won't hurt you*, she assured him again. *I'd like to be your friend. Smell me. Can you tell I understand you?*

Emily closed her eyes to repeat the words and concentrate on Midnight. His lips touched her outstretched palm.

That's it. You're starting to trust me.

She waited until he'd nuzzled her hand and arm a few times. Then she opened her eyes and met his eyes.

"Are we friends now? Can I touch you?" Emily asked.

Little by little, she turned her hand over and eased it upward until it was just over Midnight's muzzle. She hesitated there, waiting for permission. When he seemed to indicate it would be all right, she lowered her hand as lightly as a butterfly to touch his nose.

Midnight snorted and shook his head. Emily lifted her hand from his muzzle. She kept her hand

outstretched until he sniffed it. This time he acted more curious than wary.

She spoke to him again, her voice barely above a whisper. "This is a hand. You may have felt some rough hands, but mine is small. Will you let me touch you again?"

He didn't shy away from the light brush of her hand. After a few minutes, he let her set her hand on his nose. The first few times, he twisted his head away as if she were a pesky fly he was trying to dislodge. Then finally he let her set her palm down. She longed to smooth her hand along his silky muzzle but bided her time.

"Get back!" The old man's voice cracked through the stable like a whip. Emily jumped and banged her arm on the stable door.

Midnight startled and bucked and squealed. His hooves came crashing down.

The man reached Emily in several strides, wrapped his arm around her waist, and yanked her backward. He stumbled, and the two of them almost toppled to the floor. Natalie grabbed Emily's arm and steadied her until the man got his balance.

Wheezing, he let go of her, groaned, and rubbed his back. "What were you doing?" he barked. "I said stay away from the wild horses."

Crashing and banging and squealing came from Midnight's stable. Emily squeezed her eyes shut to stop the tears that threatened to overflow. She'd gotten so close. She'd almost convinced Midnight to trust her, and then she'd startled him. All that hard work destroyed with one loud yell.

"Get out of here," the man snapped.

"Wait, you don't understand," Natalie said. "My sister calmed him down. She was making friends with him."

"Friends?" the man practically spat. "Nobody makes friends with that beast."

Emily lifted her misty eyes. "He almost let me pet him."

"Almost? In a pig's eye. He probably stopped his tantrums for a second, and you stuck your hand in there." He shook his head. "What a stupid, fool thing to do."

"No." Emily's voice trembled, but she had to defend Midnight. "I talked to him. He's only scared and uneasy. He doesn't know what's happening."

"Pah. Next you'll be trying to say you're a horse whisperer."

"She might be," Natalie said. "She tamed our emu just by looking at it and talking to it. No one else could get near it."

"You have an emu?" The old man looked skeptical. "I suppose you ride it too."

"No, she just feeds and sketches it. Of course, she also plays with it." Natalie drew herself up to her full height. "Our family owns Second Chance Ranch, so we really do have an emu."

"So your mom's the vet. She has a way with animals. Maybe you do too." He didn't quite sound like he believed it. He studied Natalie's naturally tanned skin, dark hair, and brown eyes before squinting at Emily's pale skin and long blond ponytail. "You don't look like sisters."

"We are." Natalie put her arm around Emily's shoulders.

His eyes narrowed. "Well, I doubt this one inherited your mom's skills."

Emily was grateful for Natalie's closeness and coming to her defense.

"I sometimes go with Mom to help her calm down animals," Emily said. That was a bit of a stretch. She had gone two times on vet calls and had helped, but she hadn't actually been along to calm them. Mom had said she had a gift for gentling animals though.

To cover for the tears she was afraid would fall, Emily crossed her arms and tried to act brave. "That stall is too small for Midnight," she told the man.

"Midnight? Who's that?" he asked.

Emily bit her lip. "I mean, your black mustang."

"You named it already, did you? When it's not even yours?" The way the man was inspecting her made her nervous.

Emily straightened to defend herself. "I couldn't help it. I can talk to animals better when they have names."

"I see. So what exactly did *Midnight*," he stressed the name sarcastically, "tell you? What he'd prefer for a stall?"

Emily held her breath as he stared her down. She lowered her eyes. Natalie squeezed her shoulder lightly, and Emily threw her a quick thank-you glance. "Midnight would rather be home with his family in the wild," she exhaled.

She jumped at the man's deep bark of laughter. "Well, he would," he said, then shook his head. "Good guess, kid, but that's not gonna happen."

"But couldn't you give him more room? He's never been inside before." Emily couldn't believe she was saying this to the man. "He doesn't understand what's over his head. It makes him nervous."

The man crossed his arms. "Oh, really. He told you all this?"

Emily couldn't look him in the eye. "Not that part, he didn't. Not exactly." She didn't know how to explain how she knew that, but she'd sensed it. "I-I just know it. Like I know he's angry right now because we startled him." The tears she'd been holding back spilled onto her cheeks. "I'd almost convinced him I was a friend, but now I don't know if he'll ever trust me again."

"Try an apple. That always works."

The man's sarcastic response angered Emily. "That's not what he wants right now," she said.

He pulled an apple slice from his pocket. "If I give him this, he won't eat it, huh?"

"Of course he will," Emily said. "He doesn't know when he'll get food again. He'd be foolish not to take it. He's too smart to turn it down."

"You're a smart kid, but that doesn't mean I

believe you can talk to horses." The man held out the apple slice to Emily. "Here, let's see you feed this to him."

"It might take a while. He's pretty upset and scared," Emily said.

"Take your time." The man plopped down on a bale of hay, leaned his head back against the wood behind him, and stared up at the barn rafters as if he didn't care what happened.

Emily headed closer to the stall where Midnight was kicking and banging. She closed her eyes to see if he'd let her come nearer. He wasn't quite as scared as he'd been. *I'm sorry. I didn't mean to startle you like that.*

Midnight quieted a bit. He remembered her, she could tell, and he wasn't afraid of her.

Behind them, Natalie twisted her hands together. Emily could feel her sister's fear. Natalie was nervous that Emily would fail. Or get hurt. Emily glanced over her shoulder and smiled to reassure her.

She took a few more steps, and Midnight nickered. Emily smiled. He wanted to smell her again. He was curious to find out what she was. She tucked the hand with the apple behind her back and instead put out her other hand. She'd let him get used to her before she shared the apple.

Midnight pawed at the ground, impatient to examine her. Emily walked the rest of the distance.

Hay crackled as the man sat up, but Emily ignored him and extended her hand. *Here's where we were before. Can we go back to being friends?*

The man moved restlessly behind her when she slid her hand into the stall. Midnight nudged her hand as if encouraging her to touch him again. She set her hand on his muzzle and slid it a few inches down his nose. He quieted completely.

After she'd petted him a few times, she asked, "Would you like an apple?" Keeping her right hand on his nose, she brought her other hand from behind her back, inch by inch. Fear pooled in the pit of her stomach. Midnight was wild. He'd never eaten from someone's hand before. What if he bit her?

As if sensing her nervousness, he snorted, knocking her hand from his nose. Emily took some deep breaths. She couldn't let him sense she was scared. She put her right hand back on his muzzle and petted him a few more times.

"I'm a friend, and I have a treat," she whispered before sliding her left hand into his stall, palm upright, apple slice resting on it. He sniffed it, then snatched it, his teeth grazing her hand. It tickled, but Emily remained still while he nuzzled her palm.

She laughed. "I'm sorry I don't have any more, but thank you for being my friend."

Behind her, the man blew out a breath, reminding Emily that she and Midnight weren't alone in the barn. "I have to go, but it was nice to meet you," she said to Midnight. She withdrew her hands. "I did tell him you need a larger space. I have no idea if he'll listen to me, but I'll try."

She waited until she'd backed some distance from the stall before she turned. The man had risen to his feet, and Emily waited for him to kick them out of the barn.

Natalie must have had the same idea because she moved next to Emily. "Let's go, Em."

The man stared at her, assessing her with narrowed eyes. "You have a gift, kid. We might need your help around here."

Emily's eyes widened. "You mean I can help with Midnight?"

His dry chuckle sounded rusty, as if he hardly ever used it. "Doubt the boss man would go for that. How are you at mucking out stalls?"

"I do that all the time at home."

"If you're willing to do some of it here, you can stop by anytime."

"Really?" Emily stared at him.

"Yes, really." The sarcasm was back in voice.

"Duke," a voice yelled from outside, "where are you? We need you."

"Coming," he called back, but he turned to Emily. "I meant what I said. You're welcome here." Just before he exited the barn door, he turned. "If you're smart, you won't let the boss man see you go near that mustang."

Emily knew that might be a hard promise to keep, but she was so excited to spend time with Midnight, even if it was from a distance, that she nodded.

When Duke left the barn, Emily squealed and grabbed Natalie in a hug. "I can come back anytime. That's so awesome!"

Natalie's smile was a bit more cautious. "You still have chores to do at home, and just because Duke said you could come doesn't mean his boss will agree. You don't want to make a pest of yourself."

Her sister was right, but Emily couldn't hold back her excitement. She might get to spend time with and ride the wild mustang of her dreams.

Chapter Six

At dinnertime, Emily told her family about calming Midnight and his letting her pet him.

"And Duke said I could come back anytime," she finished, obviously excited.

Mr. Ramirez smiled, "Honey, the way your eyes are shining, I think you've found your gift." He turned to his wife. "Your mom's eyes shone that way when she talked about going to school to be a vet. They still do when she's talking about some of her cases."

Natalie spoke up. "That's exactly what Duke said about Emily—that she had a gift. Is it okay if I take my turn now? I want to talk about this morning too."

When Mr. Ramirez nodded, Natalie said, "Actually, this isn't exactly about me, but it made me so happy, I want to share. You know how Emily is always so shy and doesn't like to talk to people?" Natalie gave Emily an apologetic smile. "Sorry, Em, but you don't talk much."

"I know," Emily agreed.

"Anyway, Emily did a good job connecting with the mustang, but she left out the part about Duke yelling at her."

Mrs. Ramirez's eyes went wide. "Oh, girls, I hope

you didn't upset him. He can be grumpy, but he loves the horses, and he's amazing with them."

"That's what I'm trying to tell about, Mom," Natalie said.

"Oops, sorry. It wasn't my turn, but sometimes I do need to be a parent." She turned to Emily. "Please don't do anything to offend Duke."

"Mommm . . ." Natalie whined.

Mrs. Ramirez laughed. "Go ahead, Natalie. I promise not to interrupt again."

"I wanted to say how proud I was of Emily today. When Duke yelled, she stood her ground and answered him." Natalie raised her hand. "I know what you're thinking, Mom. I promise Emily was polite, but she spoke up for herself and Midnight. She was right about what she said, and she even proved it. I think he respects her now."

"Thanks, Natalie," Emily said. "You helped a lot by being there with me. I got so upset about Midnight, I forgot to be scared to talk."

"I'm not sure what to think about that," Mrs. Ramirez said. "I'm glad to hear Emily was courageous, but Rancho del Sol is one of my largest customers. I can't afford to alienate them."

"Tell her what you said, Emily, so she'll see it was all right," Natalie encouraged.

Emily ducked her head. "I don't remember. All I could think about was Midnight."

"Don't worry, Mom," Natalie said. "Emily charmed Duke the same way she charmed that horse."

"She must have if he invited her back," Mrs. Ramirez agreed. "Well, Emily, I may need to make you my assistant."

"I'd like that." Then Emily said in a quiet voice, "Um, Mom, I sort of told him a lie. I said sometimes I come along with you to calm animals. I mean, I did one or two times and helped a little, like when that goat was acting so wild."

Mrs. Ramirez thought for a moment. "You did a good job with that. I guess we'll have to make it a regular thing."

Emily felt a little better. Maybe her mom would bring her along to Rancho del Sol so Duke would see she did help. Emily had been so caught up in the conversation, she'd eaten her whole dinner without thinking about it. She hadn't even paid attention to what was on her plate.

Later, when they were in their bedroom, Grace said, "Hey, Em, it was cool you talked to that mean old man. That was really brave of you."

"He wasn't mean. I think he's just lonely." Emily wasn't sure how she knew that, but she did. She wanted to be his friend the same way she'd made friends with Midnight. She wasn't sure how to do it, but she was determined to find a way.

"Well, it sounds like you stood up for yourself."

Emily shook her head. "I was so upset about Midnight, the words just flowed out. I didn't have time to think about them."

"Maybe that's the secret," Grace said, excitedly. "Don't think about it. I don't think about things ahead of time, I just blurt them out, and I'm never scared."

Emily wasn't sure if that was the best solution. Grace had to make a lot of apologies, and she hurt people's feelings even when she didn't mean to. If she'd stop to think first, she'd have fewer misunderstandings. Emily thought too much, which was the exact opposite problem.

That night she dreamed of Midnight. The two of them galloped through the pasture, wind whipping through Emily's hair and Midnight's mane. They were wild and free.

The dream made her want to return to Rancho del Sol the next afternoon, but Emily wasn't sure she wanted to go alone. Natalie had plans with her friend Darcy and probably a lot of homework to do. Emily didn't want to ask Grace because her twin sister's impulsiveness might get them kicked off the ranch for good. Abby would be overwhelmed by all the noise and confusion. And waiting until next weekend seemed like forever.

At Sunday dinner, Emily mentioned that she wanted to see Midnight again before next weekend.

Mrs. Ramirez said, "I need to check on one of the

horses at Rancho del Sol on Tuesday night. You're welcome to ride out there with me." She shot Emily a knowing smile. "We can always say you're there as my assistant to help calm the animals."

Emily laughed. "Thanks. That would be great."

"By the way, I went to the grocery store yesterday but didn't notice until I got there that you and Grace hadn't added any ingredients to the list. Did you choose a meal yet?"

Emily and Grace looked at each other and then back at their mom, sheepishly. They had forgotten all about it.

"Oh, no. I forgot to look for a recipe," Emily said.

"I guess you'll have to make something with the ingredients we already have on hand. Be sure to find out what everyone else has planned so you don't use anything I bought for them."

"This'll be fun." Grace bounced in her chair.

Emily wasn't so sure. Yes, they'd helped their parents cook before, and sometimes she and Grace baked cookies together, but now they'd be responsible for a whole meal. And preventing Grace from creating kitchen disasters might take up a lot of her time. She was not exactly looking forward to Tuesday. At least not to the dinner part, but she was glad she'd get to see Midnight afterwards.

"Em?" Grace waved a hand in front of Emily's face. "We're going to make some great meals, right?"

"I hope so," Emily said, but doubt crept into her voice, and Grace looked as if Emily had hurt her feelings. She hadn't meant to upset her sister. "We'll do our best."

"You worry too much," Grace told her. "It'll be awesome. Wait and see."

After dinner she and Grace checked the freezer and pantry to come up with a meal idea. Mr. Ramirez was busy with the dishes, but he made several suggestions, none of which appealed to Emily.

She loved pasta, and seeing several boxes of macaroni and spaghetti on the pantry shelf gave her an idea. Dad had canned homemade tomato sauce from the tomatoes Miz Ida, their neighbor across the road, had given them before she moved. They had plenty of sauce and pasta.

Grace was snacking on a handful of breakfast cereal from the box. When Emily gave her a questioning look, she shrugged. "We didn't have dessert."

Emily swished past her. "I have an idea." She was pretty sure she'd seen frozen meatballs when they'd checked earlier. If so, that would make an easy dinner as long as they didn't let the pots overflow. "Come on."

Grace shoved the box of cereal back on the shelf without closing it.

"You should—" Before Emily could suggest shutting the box, Grace yelped.

In her haste to follow Emily, Grace hadn't set the

box far enough back on the shelf. It tipped, and cereal rained down on her head. Emily sighed.

"Oh, no." Grace crunched across the pantry floor to get the broom.

"Wait." Emily held up a hand to stop her sister. "Wouldn't it make more sense for me to get the broom? I'm right near it and have no cereal under my feet. Cleaning up whole cereal pieces is easier than if they're crushed to small crumbs."

Grace stood where she was and took the broom handle when Emily passed it to her.

After Grace had swept up most of the cereal, Emily padded over and picked up the almost-empty box. She folded the liner neatly into the box, closed the lid, and reached up to put the box on the shelf. She steadied the box with one hand until it stopped wobbling.

Then she waited while Grace returned the broom to its hook, dumped the cereal in the trash, and washed her hands. Emily was glad they weren't in a hurry to get anywhere.

After her sister returned, Emily said, "Did you ever think that if you went a little slower, you'd get done faster?"

"Huh?" Grace stared at her. "That doesn't make any sense."

"Yes, it does." Emily pointed to the cereal box. "If you'd taken a few seconds to make sure it was closed and a few more to be sure it was steady on the shelf, it would have taken maybe a half minute more than shoving it onto the shelf."

Grace frowned.

"Or with the dishes the other night," Emily continued. "If you did a quick squirt of dishwashing liquid and took two minutes to watch the sink fill . . ."

"Okay, okay. I get it," Grace said. "I'll try harder to move more slowly, but you don't know how hard it is."

"As hard as it is for me to make phone calls?" Emily asked.

"Right. I guess we all have our issues," Grace said.

Emily headed for the deep freezer. "Yep, there's a whole bag of meatballs. How does spaghetti and meatballs sound?"

"Awesome," Grace said. "I love that." Then she frowned. "What about you? You don't like it that much."

"I can have my pasta separate with butter," Emily said. The sharp taste of her dad's canned tomato sauce stung her tongue because he loaded it with onions and garlic. "I'll also keep some meatballs plain for me and Abby."

"Abby will like your way of making the meal," Grace said.

"Um, Grace," Emily said, rolling her eyes, "you should have said 'our' way. We're doing this together."

"Well, it was your idea, anyway," Grace said.

"Remember the cookies? Maybe I should watch the first few times."

Grace had set off the fire alarm when she'd burned the cookies two weeks ago.

Emily laughed and threw her arm around her sister. "Nope. It'll be you and me. Together."

As much as she loved doing things with Grace, Emily only hoped their first meal wouldn't be a total disaster.

Chapter Seven

After school on Tuesday, Emily changed out of her clothes and put on an old T-shirt and shorts. She wouldn't care if this outfit got splashed with tomato sauce. All day Monday, her mind had been filled with possible catastrophes. A smashed jar of tomato sauce splashed all over the kitchen floor. The pots boiling over and sticky pasta water and burning tomato sauce dribbling down the front of the stove. Meatballs frozen in the center. Mushy pasta.

Grace bounced into the room and dug through the piles of clothes on the floor. "Ta-da." She pulled out soccer shorts and a matching shirt.

"Shouldn't those be washed?"

"I think this pile's the clean wash." Grace pointed to the heap she'd taken her outfit from. "If not, they'll only get sweaty again, right?"

"I suppose. I hope you'll throw it in the hamper when you're done. Some stuff over there stinks." Emily pointed to several well-used, muddy soccer socks. "In fact, now might be a good time to toss those in the hamper."

Grace sighed. "I want to play soccer."

"Come on, Grace. How many minutes would it take to gather up the whole armload of wash and dump it in the bathroom hamper? If you want to practice your sprints, I'll time you."

"All right, all right. Time me starting right now." Grace scooped up a huge pile of clothes and raced to the bathroom.

"Thirteen seconds," Emily said when she returned. She reset the timer. "See if you can beat that record for another armload. One . . . two . . . three . . . go!"

Grace raced off with another load. The hamper would be overflowing. Emily wished she'd thought of this sooner. Maybe turning cleaning into a competitive sport would encourage Grace to clean up after herself.

"Ten seconds." Emily used a sports announcer voice. "And she beats the world record for laundry pickup."

Grace held her hands clasped over her head in a victory pose and turned as if there were cheering crowds in every corner of the room. "I never thought gathering up laundry could be so much fun," she said sarcastically.

"Maybe you'll do it more often," Emily said teasingly. "I can time you to see if you beat this record."

Grace wrinkled up her nose. "It's not that much fun that I'd want to do it all the time." She headed for the door. "I'd rather play soccer."

Emily laughed. "Don't forget we have to make dinner tonight."

"Ugh. Can't you do it for me?" Grace asked.

Actually, that might not be a bad idea, but her mom probably would not approve. "It's supposed to be both of us."

Grace made a face and hurried out the door.

By the time Emily had finished her homework, Mrs. Ramirez had arrived home from work.

"I took off a little early," she said. "I thought you might want a resource person in the kitchen with you, in case you have any questions."

Emily breathed a sigh of relief. Mom couldn't stop a jar of sauce from exploding if either she or Grace dropped it, but she could help to prevent cold meatballs, mushy spaghetti noodles, and pots boiling over.

When Emily called Grace into the kitchen, her sister frowned and dragged her feet, but she came.

"So what do we do first?" Grace asked.

"Why don't you get the bag of meatballs from the freezer? I'll get the pasta and sauce from the pantry." Emily headed across the kitchen. There was no way Grace could hurt frozen meatballs. At least Emily hoped not.

With Mrs. Ramirez's directions, they managed to put together the whole meal without mishaps. They even learned a trick to prevent the water in the spaghetti pot from boiling over when Mrs. Ramirez suggested they put a metal spoon in the pot. It worked well. She also suggested that Emily put the metal

colander in the sink for draining the spaghetti and stand back so the steam wouldn't burn her. Emily took charge of pouring the boiling water into the colander, while Grace opened a package and dumped some prewashed salad greens into a serving bowl.

Grace got out the salad dressing and butter. Then Emily called everyone for dinner. The whole family praised the meal. Abby was delighted to have her meatballs separate from her pasta, and so was Emily. She ate her sauce-free meatballs, buttered pasta, and salad without dressing—one of her favorite meals ever.

"I think I'm going to like cooking," she said when it was her turn to share about her day. "It was a good day today. I got an *A* on my math test, we made dinner without making any mistakes, and I'm going with Mom to Rancho del Sol after dinner."

The meal ended on a happy note because everyone had something upbeat to report. Abby took over the dishwashing, and Emily trailed her mother out to the car. She couldn't wait to see Midnight.

When Emily and her mom arrived at Rancho del Sol, a young boy led them to a different barn than the one Midnight was in. Emily tried not to act too disappointed.

"This is where we keep the horses we board," he said as he opened the barn door.

Emily wanted to ask if she could see Midnight when they were done, but her tongue stuck to the roof of her mouth. The boy was only a little older than she was. If Grace were here, she'd probably know all about him by now—how old he was, where he lived, what school he went to, what days he worked, and what his favorite sports were. Emily could barely squeak out a *hello*.

He stood and watched while Mrs. Ramirez and Emily prepared the horse for a shot. The horse was already so docile, he didn't need to be calmed. He nudged her pocket where she'd secreted some peppermints for Midnight. Emily gave him one, smoothed a hand down his neck, and whispered to him while Mrs. Ramirez worked. Emily was disappointed she wouldn't get to show Duke she acted as an assistant for her mom.

When they were done and exiting the barn, Emily looked at her mom with pleading eyes. She really wanted to see Midnight.

Mrs. Ramirez smiled at her and mouthed, *You ask.*

The words stuck in Emily's throat. How hard was it to say one sentence? Plenty hard. Scary hard. Mrs. Ramirez sent her a *you-can-do-it* look.

But she couldn't bring herself to ask. She reminded herself that she'd talked to Duke when she'd thought more about Midnight rather than focusing on herself and her own discomfort. And she remembered Grace's advice: *Don't think, just blurt it out.*

"Could we see the horses in the other barn?" Her words came out fast and all squished together.

"Huh?" The boy stopped and looked at her.

Oh, no. She'd have to repeat it with him staring at her. Emily took a deep breath and said it again. Her face heated when her voice squeaked.

The boy didn't seem to notice. "I don't know. You should ask Duke about that. He takes charge of the horses we're training."

She'd have to ask a third time? Emily wished her mom would say something, but she only reached out and squeezed Emily's hand.

"I can take you up to the barn so you can see." He changed directions and headed toward Midnight's stable.

Emily steeled herself to face Duke. He was unpredictable. Would he say *yes*?

They followed the boy up the hill to the barn door.

"Wait here," he said. Then he turned and called into the barn, "Hey, Duke? Got some people here who want to see the horses."

A loud groan came from one of the stalls. Duke emerged with a pitchfork, looking none too friendly. He scowled at Emily. His dour expression lightened a little when he looked at Mrs. Ramirez, but not by much. He rubbed his back and stared at them.

Emily struggled to ask the question, but her mouth was so dry, she couldn't form words.

Finally, he spoke in a deep, rumbly tone. "You here to muck stalls?"

Emily sent a pleading glance toward her mom. Duke was being sarcastic, but if mucking stalls would get her closer to Midnight, she'd do it.

Mrs. Ramirez looked thoughtful. "I need to go up to the house to talk to Carlos and give him my bill. We need to schedule some shots and such. You can stay for a little while."

Emily beamed at her mom. She was so thrilled, she had to restrain herself from jumping up and down.

After the boy led her mom from the barn, Emily turned and reached for the pitchfork. Duke's eyebrows rose, but he didn't say a word. He only handed it to her along with the other tools she'd need, which were leaning against the wall beside him.

She didn't speak either. Instead she went to the stall he'd emerged from and mucked it out. Natalie was a stickler for doing it right, so Emily did it as well as Natalie did it at home.

Two stalls down, Midnight was bucking and screaming. Emily longed to comfort him, but she wanted to prove herself to Duke. She tried to send Midnight calming thoughts.

I'll be there soon. You're all right.

The racket decreased a little, but she needed to be eye to eye with him. Finally, Emily couldn't bear it any longer. "Can I calm Midnight?" she asked as Duke led a horse from the stall beside Midnight's.

"Quitting already?" he said in his usual sarcastic tone.

"Of course not." Once again, he'd raised her anger and made her want to fight back.

He snorted, which might have passed for a laugh. "You planning to do the whole stable?"

"I don't have time. But I'll do as many as I can." Without waiting for his permission, she marched over to Midnight's stall and stood silent, waiting until the mustang sensed her presence.

"Midnight," she said quietly, "I have a treat for you. No, not an apple this time. Will you quiet down so I can give it to you?"

While she was talking, Mrs. Ramirez came through the door. Emily noticed her from the corner of her eye as the door banged shut, but she concentrated all her energy and attention on Midnight. She stood still and waited for him to respond. Once he did, she moved closer.

As she had the last time, Emily slowly slipped her hand into the stall until she could touch Midnight's muzzle and stroke it. Then she slipped a hand into her pocket and brought out the peppermint. She eased it toward the horse.

Midnight drew back his head the first time she brought it near his nose, but then he came closer and scooped it up, his breath warm on her hand. He scarfed down two more peppermints.

"Sorry, that's all I have," Emily said. "Will you be good so I can finish mucking out stalls?" When Midnight tossed his head and neighed, Emily laughed. "You promise?" He neighed again.

As Emily moved away from the stall, Mrs. Ramirez breathed out a loud sigh of relief.

Duke snorted. "She's got wild horses eating out of her hand."

"She certainly does," Mrs. Ramirez agreed.

"Mom, I promised to muck out the stalls," Emily said. "Is it okay for me to stay until I finish?"

"I don't know. I have a lot of paperwork to complete tonight," Mrs. Ramirez said.

"Can I at least do Midnight's?" Emily pleaded.

Mrs. Ramirez rubbed a finger across her lips. Then she looked at Duke. He shrugged.

"All right."

When Duke approached Midnight's stall to take him out, the horse started acting up.

"Can I do it?" Emily asked.

Duke stepped back, a sour expression on his face. "Be my guest."

When she opened the stall door, Midnight charged out and raced around down the barn aisle, eyes rolling. Mrs. Ramirez flattened herself against the wall, and Duke let himself into the nearest stall.

"Get in his stall, Emily, and shut the door before he turns around." Mrs. Ramirez barked the command.

"He'll be all right," Emily assured her mother. "Let him run a bit. He's been cooped up."

"A barn aisle isn't a place for running," Mrs. Ramirez said in a worried voice.

"Please," Emily pleaded. "Just give him a few minutes."

Midnight kicked and bucked and snorted and charged from one end of the barn to the other. After a few minutes, Emily stepped away from the wall, holding a lead rope.

"I know it's scary," she said and held out her other hand, wishing she had another peppermint.

Midnight ignored her as he made two more wild circuits around the barn. Emily waited for the right moment and then stepped into his path when he was half a barn-length away.

Mrs. Ramirez screamed, but Midnight slowed and stopped.

Emily clipped on the lead rope and tied Midnight

outside the stall. "I'm sorry to do this to you, but I don't want anyone to get hurt."

Midnight snorted and pulled against the rope. His sides were heaving from the run and from fear.

"It won't be long, I promise." She scratched him on his withers, and he lowered his head. Their ponies liked that, but Emily hadn't been sure if a wild horse would like it too. Evidently he did.

She took care of his stall, untied the lead rope, and led him back into the stall. After scratching him again, she removed the rope and left the stall. "Be a good boy," she told him as she closed and locked the stall door.

She handed the tools back to Duke. "I guess mucking's hard when your back hurts."

His shaggy eyebrows rose. "How'd you know that?"

She shrugged. "I can tell." She'd seen his grimaces when he moved, heard his groan earlier, and seen him rubbing his back. Most of all, she'd sensed it.

"So you're a people whisperer too, eh?" Duke said.

Emily wasn't sure about that. All she knew was that because she was so quiet, she'd spent a lot of time observing people and listening—not just to their words but to their inflections, their pauses, their body movements, their actions. Often what was unsaid was more important than what was said. She'd learned to read people and animals.

On their way out of the barn, Mrs. Ramirez said,

"Your sister was right when she said you have a gift, but unless you agree to some basic safety rules, you won't be coming back here again. What you did tonight was much too dangerous. I was really afraid you were going to get seriously injured, Emily."

From the minute they got into the car until they arrived at the house, Mrs. Ramirez hammered home the safety precautions she expected Emily to follow. "I've always had to lecture Grace on safety, not you," she said. "You've always been dependable, thoughtful. You think before you act. But if you're going to allow your love for wild horses to overrule common sense, you will not be visiting Rancho del Sol again."

Mrs. Ramirez blew out a long, exasperated breath. "I'm positive your dad will back me up on this. If I hear you've broken one of these rules, we will not allow you to bid on another wild mustang. Do you understand me?"

Emily understood perfectly. If she followed her instincts and did what she knew the horse wanted or needed, she'd break many of the precautions her mother had listed. How could she stop doing what was right for Midnight? But if she didn't obey the rules, she'd never get a mustang of her own.

Chapter Eight

Early the next Saturday morning, Emily's parents dropped her off at the ranch before they went to town to run errands and do the grocery shopping. Her sisters had agreed to do her chores for the day so she could see Midnight. Or rather, so she could help muck out stalls at Rancho del Sol. But what she really wanted was to see Midnight again.

"Call us when you're ready to come home," Mr. Ramirez said as the car bounced along the rutted driveway toward the barns. "We'll be back from town around one or so, but you can stay longer if you'd like."

"I'm hoping to stay all day. Could someone come to get me before dinner?"

"Let's make sure they're all right with that first." Mr. Ramirez pulled to a stop several yards from the barn.

Emily gasped. Midnight and another mustang, a chestnut, were running in the circular corral. Midnight's black mane and tail were blowing in the breeze. Emily could sit here and watch forever.

Midnight must be thrilled to be in a larger space, Emily thought. The corral was nothing like roaming the open range, but having a companion and an opportunity to run after being cooped up in a small stall must feel heavenly. Emily wouldn't interrupt his freedom. He needed this chance to exercise.

Some of the other horses had been turned out to pasture. They nipped at each other, nibbled grass, played together, and flicked flies away with their tails. None of them had the exuberance and joy of the two mustangs.

"Emily?" Mrs. Ramirez said. "We need to get going. Why don't you check to see how long you can stay?"

With fear in the pit of her stomach, Emily dragged her feet on the way to the barn. If Duke wasn't there, who would she have to talk to?

The minute she opened the barn door, Duke turned his head. "You again?"

His dismissive tone made Emily feel as if she were a piece of chewed gum stuck to his shoe that he couldn't remove.

Emily choked up. She'd come to help, but he didn't want her here. Despite his gruffness, though, she felt sorry for him. The tightness around his eyes and mouth showed he was holding back pain. "Are you all right?"

He ignored her question.

Emily stood her ground. "I came to see Midnight, but I can help muck out stalls."

At that, he turned around and crossed his arms, massaging his elbows, as he stared her down. Emily felt as if he were testing her to see if she would crack under pressure. Although it was hard for her, she maintained eye contact.

He waved a hand toward the stalls. "So what're you standing around for? Get to work."

"Yes, sir," Emily managed to say. "My parents need to know when to pick me up."

One side of his lip quirked at the word *sir*, but his expression remained stern and forbidding. He flapped a hand. "How should I know? Whenever you're ready to go."

Emily ran out to the car. "I think I can stay, but I'll call you if that changes."

Mrs. Ramirez handed her a lunch bag. "Here are some snacks, a lunch, and a bottle of water. That should hold you."

"Thanks, Mom. I'll see you both later," Emily said, waving good-bye to her parents.

Although the overcast sky made the day look dreary, Emily's heart was filled with sunshine. Not about mucking out the stable but because she'd have time around Midnight. She practically skipped to the barn.

Setting her lunch on a high shelf, she grabbed the tools and headed for the first stall.

"How many are you planning to do?" a gruff voice asked behind her.

"All of them," Emily said.

"Hmmph." Duke was a man of few words.

Emily turned to face him. "You look like you're in pain."

"Perceptive, aren't you?" When she didn't answer, he said, "Arthritis acts up real bad in this kind of weather."

"I thought so," Emily said.

"Now you're going to claim you can diagnose ill-nesses?" Duke grumbled.

Emily let out a small giggle. "Not yet. Maybe when I'm older. I just meant you seemed . . ." She couldn't say grumpy, even though that's how he was acting. "Um . . ."

"Testy? Crotchety? Mean?" Duke offered.

"No. Stiff and sore," Emily said.

"Oh, go on with you." Duke waved her away. "Get the stalls done."

"Yes, sir," Emily said. "Right away, sir." He seemed to like that earlier. This time he almost cracked a smile.

Rancho del Sol's stables were at least three times larger than their stables at home. Emily's arms and back ached, and sweat poured down her brow by the time she stopped for lunch. She sat on the wall outside the barn door where she had a good view of Midnight. Duke hadn't eaten anything or taken any breaks.

"Aren't you going to eat lunch?" she called to him.

"Too much to do," Duke called back.

"You should have something," Emily called, alarmed. No wonder he was grumpy. "Do you like peanut butter?"

Duke stopped what he was doing to come closer to her. He peered at her suspiciously. "Why?"

"Because that's what I brought for lunch." Emily reached into the lunch bag, unwrapped her sandwich, and held out half.

"I don't need it," he snapped.

Emily didn't want to hurt his pride by insisting he take it, but she set it on a napkin on the wall between them and pushed it in his direction.

He waved a hand toward the sandwich. "You eat that."

"Everyone should have lunch." Emily dug in her bag and split the cookies, leaving two in the plastic bag she pushed in his direction and eating one. She peeled her orange, broke it in half, and set one half on top of the cookie bag. Then she hopped off the wall with the small bag of apple slices.

"Hey, wait," Duke called after her. "Where are you going?"

"To watch Midnight for a little bit," Emily said over her shoulder. "Don't worry. I'll finish the work."

She walked toward the corral, figuring if she didn't look at Duke, he'd eat the food.

Midnight whinnied and slowed his galloping as Emily approached. The other mustang followed his lead. Midnight threw back his head and snorted. Then he headed in her direction. Emily was thrilled. He remembered her.

The other mustang hung back, but Midnight came close to the corral fence. After letting him nuzzle her arm, she patted him and fed him some apple slices.

"I wish I could stay longer," Emily told the horse, "but I need to finish the stalls."

When she returned to the barn, the food she'd left had disappeared. She hoped Duke had eaten it and not thrown it in the trash. She wondered if he ate regular meals. That might explain some of his orneriness.

A radio blasted a football game as she entered the barn. Maybe he was hard of hearing too. Or perhaps he had as much trouble talking to people as she did, so he wanted to fill the silence. One thing that puzzled her was how she'd talked to him when she was usually shy around people when she first met them. Maybe it was because she sensed his loneliness and hurt.

While she mucked, Duke brought in the horses one by one and groomed them before returning them to their stalls. Emily admired their gleaming coats. She had no idea how he managed all this work by himself. He must have others who helped him. She'd practically have to yell to carry on a conversation, so she couldn't ask him.

The next time he went outside, Duke stopped in the doorway. "I don't like the looks of that sky. Let's get the horses inside." He spoke loudly enough to be heard over the radio announcer's patter.

Emily stared out the open door. The sky had darkened. Winds whipped the horses' manes and chased clouds into frantic movement. The air around them had a strange greenish-yellow cast, and in the distance, heavy gray clouds massed close to the horizon.

"Finish mucking out that last stall," he yelled. "I'm going to warn the others." As the door closed behind him, he called over his shoulder, "And turn down that dang-fool radio."

Emily wanted to retort she wasn't the one who had turned it on in the first place, but the door slammed behind him. She'd be happy to turn the noise off. She had to climb on some hay bales to reach the shelf. Right before she clicked it off, she heard the football game announcer say, "Tornado warning in effect until 3:30 p.m."

She jumped off the bale and raced for the exit, almost hitting Duke in the face with the door.

"Tornado warning," she told him, all out of breath.

"No need to screech." He continued to lead several horses into the barn. "Get that last stall mucked out, and get the wheelbarrow and tools put away. Someone went to warn them at the house. They'll be down to help too. The twister might pass us by, but better to be safe than sorry."

Emily rushed into the last stall and finished

cleaning it. Then she ran to the barn door to see what she could do. She wished she were home, helping her family. Had they even heard the news?

Pulling her cell phone from her pocket, she called the Second Chance Ranch barn. Grace answered. "Did you get the tornado warning?" Emily asked.

"Yes, we're busy getting all the animals inside. Can't talk now," Grace said, breathing heavily.

From a distance, her mom shouted to Grace, and Grace yelled back. Then she said, "Mom says to go into the tornado shelter there. They won't come to pick you up until after it's over. Be safe."

"You too." Tears welled in Emily's eyes. She didn't want to be in a tornado shelter with strangers. She wanted to be with her family. Grace hung up the phone before Emily could say good-bye.

In the pasture, ranch hands were rounding up horses and leading them to the different barns. Emily went down to help. She passed the corral as one of the men prepared to lasso Midnight, who screamed and bucked as the man approached the fence with the rope.

"This one will be a challenge," he said.

"Don't do that," Emily yelled, surprising herself and the man. "You're frightening him. Can't you see he's scared and upset?"

"Get out of the way," the man said angrily. "This is a dangerous job."

Duke passed nearby with two horses. Emily called out to him. "Duke, please make him stop. I can get Midnight to behave."

"Hey, Carlos, let the girl take that wild one in," Duke said. "She might surprise you."

Carlos looked at Duke as if he were crazy. "Don't be ridiculous. Nobody can get near him."

"Just let her try," Duke said.

"No way." Carlos shook his head. "Her parents would sue me if anything happened to her."

Sue him? He must be the owner of Rancho del Sol, Emily realized, and she'd just yelled at him to leave his own horse alone. Emily hoped Mom wouldn't lose his business, but she couldn't stand by and watch him upset Midnight.

"Trust me on this, Carlos. Move everyone away and let her stand outside the corral." Duke handed the reins of the two horses he was holding to one of the stable boys hurrying from the barn. "Start putting on the breakaway halters," Duke ordered the boy.

Just then the tornado warning siren split the air. Midnight grew even more unruly.

Emily had to find a way to reach him, to calm him down. She headed for the fence. If he could see her, maybe it would help.

"Don't go in there!" Carlos screamed.

Duke came over and set a hand on his arm. "The girl is a horse whisperer. Watch and see."

"We don't have time. The siren's going off. That gives us a ten- or twelve-minute warning." Carlos pointed toward the funnel of gray clouds swirling in a distance.

Emily blocked out their conversation. She blocked out the roar of the wind. She blocked out the ominous clouds forming on the horizon. She blocked out the hailstones falling around her, hitting her. They barely registered because she'd focused her mind and senses on one thing, and only one thing: saving Midnight.

Chapter Nine

Emily jogged around the outside of the corral fence so she could face Midnight. She wanted to go in but worried Carlos might yell at her or stop her and make Midnight's fear worse. With the siren blaring in Midnight's sensitive ears, she couldn't talk to him with words. She had to reach him and get him inside the barn before the tornado hit.

It's all right, Midnight. I want to help you.

The siren died. In that quiet, with her ears still ringing from the noise, she called to Midnight. His hooves struck the ground, and his ears flicked back and forth anxiously. With his legs splayed and his body leaning back, he looked ready to bolt.

"Wait, Midnight," Emily called.

He looked in her direction, his nostrils flaring and his eyes darting from side to side. After he focused on her, he turned his ears forward.

"Come with me," she said, holding out her hand but standing in place. Midnight's body was quivering. "I know you're scared. Can you feel the tornado approaching?" Emily continued talking softly, gently. She coaxed him toward her.

When he reached her, she ran her tense fingers down his nose, letting the softness of his muzzle soothe her own frazzled nerves as she tried to calm him. Now that she had his attention, she had to lead him out of here and up to the barn. Would he cooperate and go inside that tiny stall again?

She'd been so busy concentrating on Midnight, she hadn't paid attention to the chestnut, who'd followed Midnight's lead and stopped bucking. The chestnut was pawing the ground nearby. Emily hoped he'd follow Midnight when she led him to the gate. Maybe Carlos could lasso him and get him to his stall.

Emily tilted her head in the direction she wanted Midnight to go, and she shuffled toward the gate. Midnight stayed with her, so she picked up her pace until the two of them were racing for the gate. The chestnut thundered after him.

Suddenly a clap of thunder erupted and a burst of lightning lit the sky, startling both horses. They both skidded to a stop, their terror showing in their eye rolls and trembling bodies.

Please stay with me, Midnight.

She caught his attention and moved him forward. They'd almost reached the gate. Duke had moved Carlos up the hill by the barn. Emily glanced at Duke to be sure Carlos wouldn't come charging down after them, scaring both horses even more.

Emily tensed as she got ready to open the gate. What if the mustangs chose to escape? She had no way to catch them. She reached for the latch on the gate. Once she opened it, she'd have no control over Midnight's choices.

"Please don't bolt," she whispered over and over. He couldn't hear her over the siren, which had begun to blare again, but she hoped he could interpret her body language and understand her nonverbal message.

She eased the gate open, dread pooling in her stomach as she pulled it wide enough for the mustangs to exit. For a few seconds, Midnight appeared ready to flee, but then he lowered his head and walked beside her up the path to the barn. She scratched his withers to reward him for cooperating, and then she placed a comforting hand on his neck to guide him up to the barn.

Duke and Carlos moved away to give Midnight a wide berth. Both men stared at Emily, making her nervous. But she closed her mind to them, pretending they weren't there. Her focus needed to be on Midnight. She wouldn't waver until she had gotten him safely into his stall.

The way up to the barn went smoothly, with Midnight cooperating and the chestnut imitating Midnight's every move. At the stable door, Midnight balked and refused to enter. Emily pleaded with him in a whisper, sending messages to encourage him to cross the threshold.

She patted his neck, trying not to let her fear and tension show.

We need to hurry. It's dangerous out here. Please, please come with me.

Midnight took a hesitant step in her direction. She moved him forward and entered his stall. He poked his head inside and shook his head, letting her know he didn't want to go back into that tiny box again.

The tornado was approaching. She had to get him to come the whole way inside.

Duke came through the barn door with a lariat in his hands. He tossed the lariat over the chestnut's neck and pulled, startling Midnight, who bolted forward. As soon as Midnight cleared the stall door and before he could turn and escape, Emily slammed and locked the door. Except now she was stuck inside with him.

Midnight pawed the ground, then turned around and around as if looking for an opening to escape. Finding none, his eyes rolled back until the whites were showing. He trembled and snorted.

Duke wrestled the chestnut into a stall, and Carlos struggled to put a breakaway halter on him. Other horses were restless in their stalls. The siren covered most of the noise, but the sense of approaching danger hung over them.

Midnight would never let her put a breakaway halter on him, but the phone number on the halter was the only way to find any horses that happened to get loose during the storm.

"A grease pencil," Emily yelled to Duke.

Duke reached into his pocket and tossed her one. She didn't know Rancho del Sol's phone number, so she started to write her home number on Midnight's side with the white pencil. Midnight snorted and backed away. She scratched his withers with her left hand to calm him while she wrote, but he continued to wriggle until she finished.

A loud clatter on the roof startled her, and she jumped. The tornado was close enough to start throwing debris around. Midnight pawed the ground, then spread his legs in a wider stance and leaned back as if preparing to buck.

No, Midnight, please.

If he kicked and bucked with her in this tiny stall, she'd be crushed. She tried to convey that she understood his fear. He was trapped and terrified, so it was his instinct.

"Come on!" Duke yelled. "We have to get out of here."

Sending Midnight calming mental messages, she eased toward the door. When she unlatched it and walked out, Midnight went berserk. Bucking and kicking, he battered the stall walls. Was he trying to tell her he wanted to get out too?

Emily been through tornadoes before with their

own horses, and Natalie had told her horses often can sense disaster. At Second Chance Ranch, they let their horses choose where to go during a storm or tornado because they believed the animals had good instincts. Most cooperated and went into the barn. If they didn't, Natalie tried to listen to them and figure out what they wanted.

Duke had finished and was waiting for her by the barn door. "Come on," he screamed. "We're running out of time!"

Emily was going to follow her own instincts and give Midnight the chance to choose. She left the door unlatched and slightly ajar. Then she dashed to where Duke was waiting. She hoped he couldn't tell what she'd done. She also prayed Midnight would wait until they exited the barn to break free.

"Hurry," Duke said.

Stones and small flying debris pelted Emily, stinging her arms and face, though Duke tried to shelter her with his body. He put an arm around her shoulders to keep her from blowing away in the strong, gale-force winds, and together they raced for safety.

Duke yanked open the shelter door, and a blast of air shoved them inside. The force of the wind slammed the heavy door shut behind them with a loud bang, and Emily jumped.

When they climbed down into the shelter, Emily hung back. So many people packed together in a dim,

sunless space. A radio blared the news, tracing the path of the tornado as it barreled toward the ranch.

Emily hoped her family and all the animals were safe. She wished she were in their small tornado shelter rather than this huge one. She and her sisters had old board games stored down there. They'd play games and listen to the radio. This was a time to be surrounded by people she loved, not complete strangers. At least she didn't have to worry about making conversation. Everyone listened to the radio with rapt attention.

After a half hour of waiting, listening to the screaming wind and thudding of falling objects, Emily heard the radio announce the storm had passed several miles to the east of Sugarberry and had now reached another county. Emily hoped that meant their ranch, which was to the west of town, was safe.

They emerged to find wreckage had littered the ground, and a fallen tree had crashed through the barn roof. Emily screeched and raced toward the stable. The others pounded alongside her.

"Don't go in there," Duke shouted at her. "The roof could collapse." He started barking orders to other stable hands. He formed one group to let the horses out and another to gather material to stabilize the roof and patch it temporarily.

Emily ignored his warning and flung open the

barn door. The tree had fallen directly over Midnight's stall. It had crushed the wood.

"Midnight," she screamed. His stall was empty. There was no sign of him anywhere.

At the opposite end of the barn, the door creaked back and forth. In their rush to get the last two horses into the barn, they'd forgotten to latch it. Midnight had escaped.

"What do you think you're doing?" Duke snapped, startling Emily. She hadn't realized he had entered

the barn. "Get out of there this instant. It's much too dangerous in here. We don't want you getting hurt."

Emily obeyed. "Midnight isn't in his stall," she said as she passed him. "He's gone."

Duke flapped a hand. "You put a number on him, right?" When she nodded, he said, "Don't worry. He'll turn up."

Emily pulled out her phone to call her parents. She grew teary-eyed when her mom answered. They'd had some minor damage to the barn, and one side of the pasture fence had been destroyed. Several trees had been uprooted, but other than smashing one window in the small storage shed, the trees had all fallen in the pasture or the side yard.

While she waited for her mom to pick her up, Emily watched the stable hands turning the horses out to pasture. Her heart ached that Midnight was not among them, but she was glad she'd left his stall door open. Midnight must have sensed the danger. That's why he threw such a fit. Except now he was missing.

Chapter Ten

After Midnight disappeared, Emily moved through her days like a robot, not feeling, not reacting. She dressed for school, sat in classes, scribbled answers on tests and homework, did her chores, ate her meals, and put one foot in front of the other to move from place to place. But nothing penetrated the thick covering she'd put over her heart. No feelings could come in, and no feelings could go out. Nothing touched her.

After two weeks had passed with no sign of Midnight, everyone insisted he'd escaped and gone back to the wild. Somewhere out there, a mustang ran wild on the range, kicking up his heels in joy at no longer being confined in a tiny wooden box, no longer trapped in a stall.

On his side, he had white markings—their phone number. How long would the grease pencil stay on if Midnight rolled in the grass and dirt, got drenched in thunderstorms, or swam across rivers? Would the numbers fade quickly? And when they did, would Midnight's memories of her fade too? The thought of him being free made Emily happy, but her heart ached to know she'd never see him again.

One Saturday morning after she'd done her chores, again by rote, Emily slumped on the couch.

She couldn't even muster up the energy to turn on the TV. Her books lay unread on the table by her bed. She hadn't picked up her paints or her camera. Every time she looked through the lens, she thought of Midnight and wished she'd taken a picture so she had something to remember him.

Maybe she could find his picture online at the auction site. Did they keep pictures of sold horses? She had just reached the site when the phone rang. She ignored it, and it stopped. Then it rang again, right away.

"Can someone get that?" Natalie called from the kitchen where she was baking cookies.

Emily only stared at the phone.

With a huff, Natalie hurried down the hall. She sent Emily a sidelong glance but didn't scold her. Everyone in the family understood her aversion to phones, and Natalie had been especially nice about Midnight going missing.

"Hello," Natalie said, a bit of exasperation in her voice. "Oh, hi, Marco." Her face and posture changed to perky to match her tone, which now also dripped sweetness.

Emily was pretty sure Natalie had a crush on Marco, whose family owned the ranch next door.

"A black horse?" Natalie asked. "With our phone number on it?"

"Our phone number?" Emily struggled to process

what her sister said. She whispered to Natalie, "Marco saw a black horse with our phone number?"

Natalie nodded to Emily, her eyes wide. "Okay, we'll be right over to get him," she said to Marco.

As soon as she hung up, Natalie squealed. "The Cruzes can't catch Midnight, but I'm sure you can coax him." When Emily didn't move, Natalie grabbed her hand and tugged her off the couch. "Em, are you all right?"

"I-I don't know." Emily was still too dazed to think straight.

Natalie clapped her hands in front of Emily's face. "Wake up. Midnight needs you."

Her sister had said the magic words: *Midnight needs you*. Emily shook herself as if she were waking from a deep sleep, one filled with nightmares about Midnight being missing. She had that groggy, just-woken-up feeling, not sure if the news was even real.

"Let's go." Natalie started toward the door. "Oh, wait. The cookies and . . ."

It took Natalie more than ten minutes to take the cookies out of the oven and change her outfit and brush her hair and put on lip gloss and pack some cookies for Marco. By the time she was ready, Emily had processed the news and couldn't wait to get going. She'd told the rest of the family, and everyone was as excited as she was.

Emily nagged at Natalie the whole time. "What if Midnight runs off while you're packing cookies and putting on lip gloss?" She'd already stuffed her pockets with apples and peppermints. That was all the preparation she needed.

"All right, all right, I'm ready." Natalie took one last glance at herself in the mirror, smoothed down her hair, and picked up the small bag of cookies.

When they reached the Cruzes' ranch, Natalie

simpered and asked Marco where Midnight was. He pointed to a black blur just beyond the tree line. When Emily headed toward the mustang, Marco turned his attention to Natalie.

Emily tried to connect her mind with Midnight's. She tuned in to him as she walked in his direction. Her heart called out to him to stay where he was and not run. With each step she took, her excitement built. They'd be together again.

"Midnight," she called, praying he'd recognize her voice and not blame her for the tree and the tornado.

He twitched and looked startled, but he didn't take off. She hoped that was a good sign. He watched her as she got closer. Emily stopped a few yards away. She wanted to see if he'd come to her.

Holding out a hand, she met his eyes and waited. He snorted and stamped, and Emily listened. Then he took a step toward her. And another.

Emily couldn't wait any longer. She hurried to him, pulling an apple slice from the small plastic bag in her pocket. She held it out, and he ate it. After three apple slices and one peppermint, she started leading him toward their house. She waved to Natalie, who was too engrossed in talking to Marco to notice.

By continuing to feed Midnight bits of food, Emily got him home and into an empty stall in the barn. The rest of the family watched from the kitchen window.

They cheered from behind the glass when Emily emerged from the barn.

Emily wished she could keep Midnight, but he wasn't hers. She had to make a phone call. She went into the house to get Rancho del Sol's business card. With shaky hands, she dialed the number. Her voice trembled when she told Carlos she'd found Midnight. He said he'd be right over. After she hung up, she crumpled onto the couch. She could still go to the ranch to see Midnight, but now that she had him in a stall in the barn, it would be hard to return him to his owner.

She went out to the barn to wait and spend more time with Midnight. First she fed him, then she reached into the stall to pet him.

Mr. Ramirez entered the barn. "You seem to have an amazing connection to that horse."

Emily's lip trembled. "I wish I could keep him."

"I know." Her dad approached slowly and put an arm around her.

Midnight snorted and backed away from Emily, but he didn't buck. Maybe he was getting used to people. Gravel crunched in the driveway, signaling Midnight's owner had arrived.

"I'll wait outside," Mr. Ramirez said, "so I don't spook Midnight."

Carlos backed his horse trailer up to the barn, and Emily led Midnight toward it. The mustang balked before going up the ramp. Duke stood on one side and Carlos on the other. As soon as Midnight saw them, his nostrils flared and he snorted, signs he was getting ready to throw a fit. Emily could calm him and convince him to walk into the trailer, but she didn't want to let him go.

Gathering her courage, she asked, "Could I buy him?"

Carlos shook his head, but Duke intervened. "Why not let her? That horse is a lot of trouble."

Carlos pursed his lips. "How much are you willing to pay?"

She looked at her dad, and he nodded. Emily named the sum her parents had given her for the top bid.

"Sorry, but he's worth a lot more than that." Carlos motioned for her to load Midnight into the trailer.

"Wait a minute," Duke said. "We can't sell a horse if no one can ride it. What about letting her work off the rest of the price? I can vouch that she's good at mucking out stalls. Maybe she could use her horse-whispering skills to help us train other wild mustangs."

Carlos rubbed his chin. "She does seem to have a gift for that." He stood silent for a few moments, looking from Emily to Midnight to his empty horse trailer. "All right, it's a deal, if your parents will let you help out at the ranch two hours a week."

"Dad?" Emily turned to her father expectantly. He had to agree. He just had to.

"Well," Mr. Ramirez said, "Emily has a lot of chores here at our ranch." He looked thoughtful. "But I know how much she loves this horse. If she's willing to put in the time after her chores and homework are done, she has our permission."

"I'll do all my chores and homework first, I promise," Emily assured her dad. "Thank you, thank you," she said to him and to Carlos and Duke.

Then she buried her face in Midnight's mane He was really, truly hers! She'd found the horse of her dreams. Midnight nickered and leaned closer to Emily. She knew exactly what he was thinking. He'd found the perfect home.

About the Author

When she was young, Laurie J. Edwards brought home many stray dogs and cats. She told her mother they just followed her home, but pieces of leftover meat from her lunch also might have helped to attract them. The pet she wanted most, though, was a horse. Her parents insisted their yard was too small. When she turned thirteen, Laurie began taking riding lessons and spent as much time as she could around horses.

She grew up and became a librarian because she loved books as much as she loved animals. Then she discovered the joys of writing books as well as reading them. Now she is the author of more than 40 books.

About the Illustrator

Jomike Tejido is an author and illustrator who has illustrated the books *I Funny: School of Laughs* and *Middle School: Dog's Best Friend*, as well as the Pet Charms and I Want to Be . . . Dinosaurs! series. He has fond memories of horseback riding as a kid and has always liked drawing fluffy animals. Jomike lives in Manila with his wife, his daughter Sophia, and a chow chow named Oso.

Join Natalie, Abby, Emily, and Grace and
read more animal stories in . . .

BY KELSEY ABRAMS

ILLUSTRATED BY JOMIKE TEJIDO

CHARMING MIDDLE GRADE FICTION
FROM JOLLY FISH PRESS